Something

SCARY

Other titles by Patricia Hermes
you will enjoy:

My Secret Valentine
Turkey Trouble
Christmas Magic

Something SCARY

Patricia Hermes

Illustrated by
John Steven Gurney

A
LITTLE APPLE
PAPERBACK

SCHOLASTIC INC.
New York Toronto London Auckland Sydney

ISBN 0-590-50963-2

Copyright © 1996 by Patricia Hermes. All rights reserved. Published by Scholastic Inc. LITTLE APPLE PAPERBACKS is a trademark of Scholastic Inc.

12 11 10 9 8 7 6 5 4 3 2 1   6 7 8 9/9 0 1/0

Printed in the U.S.A.   40

First Scholastic printing, September 1996

For Jessica Camille Hermes and
Samuel James Hermes

Contents

1

A Secret

"Look at this, Obie!" Katie Potts said to her twin brother, Obidiah. She bent and picked up a leaf that had blown against the school-yard fence. It was a big red maple leaf. "Isn't it beautiful?" she said.

"Look at mine," Obie said. "Mine's beautiful, too."

He held up his great big yellow leaf in front of his face.

"It's as big as your head," Katie said.

"Does it hide my ears?" Obie said.

"Yup," Katie said.

"Dumb ears," Obie said. He sighed.

"They're nice ears," Katie said.

She knew that Obie thought his ears were too big. He was always trying to press them in, one hand on either side of his head. Katie thought that maybe his ears were a little big, but not extra big or anything.

After a minute, Obie took the leaf away from his face and bent over to pick up more leaves.

Mrs. Henry, their teacher, had told everybody in class to collect leaves, as many different kinds and colors as they could. They were going to make leaf books, leaf cards, or leaf decorations, anything they wanted. Mrs. Henry said it was a fun thing to do in the fall.

Katie was tired of leaf things, though. She wanted to think of something much more fun for fall. She wanted to think about Halloween. And the Halloween secret that her best friend, Amelia, had told her.

Katie looked around the school yard, trying to find Amelia.

Amelia was under the huge oak tree, also picking up leaves.

Amelia saw Katie and waved at her.

Katie waved back. Then she began to sing a song to herself. "Secret, secret, secret," she sang. "Amelia and me have a secret. Secret, secret, secret."

Obie kept digging through the leaf pile.

"Secret, secret, secret," Katie sang a little louder.

Obie stood up. He held his leaves together by the stems like a bunch of flowers.

He put a big purple one in his leaf bouquet, and a little purple one next to it. "What secret?" he said.

"Just a secret," Katie said.

Obie frowned and looked down at his sneakers. "That's mean," he said.

Katie looked at her bunch of leaves. She picked out a red one with no spots on it and no holes in it. She gave it to Obie.

"Here," she said. "You don't have any red."

Obie put the red one with the others. "It's still mean," he said.

"Promise you won't tell?" Katie asked.

"I won't tell," Obie said.

"It's a party," Katie said. "A Halloween party."

Obie frowned. "But Mom said no Halloween party this year. She and Daddy are going to their convention this week, remember? And Grandma and Grandpa are coming to take care of us, remember?"

"I remember," Katie said. "But it's not my party. It's Tiffany's. She's having a party."

Obie scraped some mud off one foot with the other one. "You had a fight with Tiffany," he said "You called her a big pig."

"She's not too much like a pig," Katie said. "And you know what? She already invited Amelia and Susan and Jessica and Mary."

"Did she invite you?" Obie asked.

"She will," Katie said. She twisted a

leaf around by the stem, twirling it. "She has to."

"How come?" Obie said.

"Remember?" Katie said. "It's Mrs. Henry's rule. If you pass out invitations in school, you have to invite everyone. Girls have to ask all the girls, and boys have to ask all the boys."

Obie made his face into a big frown, the way he did when he was thinking hard.

He looked at his watch. He was always looking at his watch. It was his favorite thing, maybe because he was always worried about being on time. "Let's get in line," he said. "The bell's going to ring soon."

Katie twirled her leaf again. She pretended it was a magic wand.

"Katie?" Obie said. "What if Tiffany doesn't give out the invitations in school? What if she gives them out somewhere else?"

Katie shrugged. "She won't," she said. "Amelia got hers on the school bus and that's almost like school."

"Not exactly," Obie said.

"Almost," Katie said.

The bell rang loudly.

It meant that recess was over and they had to line up. Two by two. And no talking.

Katie waved her magic wand again. She did it quietly. She was a fairy leading the line, a fairy with a magic wand.

"But what if she doesn't?" Obie whispered.

"She will," Katie said.

She crossed her fingers.

She waved her magic wand.

And she hoped.

No Invitations

All the way into school, Katie twirled her magic leaf wand. Party, party, party, she thought. Tiffany will invite me to her party.

When she got to class, she walked very slowly past Tiffany's desk. She took eentsy, teentsy steps. Tiffany would look up and see her. And then she'd remember about the invitation.

Tiffany did look up and see her. She made a big mad huffy breath. Maybe she remembered being called a big pig.

Katie made herself smile at Tiffany anyway, but her lips felt stiff.

Party, party, party, she thought.

Tiffany made another huffy breath, even louder, then bent to look inside her desk.

Katie frowned at the back of Tiffany's head.

Then she slid into her seat beside Amelia.

"Did she?" Amelia said. "Did she ask you?"

"No," Katie said.

"Oh," Amelia said.

"She probably just forgot," Katie said.

"Probably," Amelia said.

"All right, class," Mrs. Henry said then. "Time to work on our leaf collections. The glue and the tracing paper are up here. Who would like to pass out the construction paper?"

"I'm the paper person this week!" Katie said. "Remember?"

"That's right, you are!" Mrs. Henry said.

She smiled at Katie. "You give out the

paper, then. Each person can pick the color paper they want. But remember, the person who hands out the papers has to choose last."

"I remember," Katie said. She went up front and took the pile of construction paper.

There were blue papers and green ones and brown ones and yellow ones. There were gray ones, too—yucky, yucky gray ones. There were only three red ones, though.

Katie wanted red. She slid a red one onto the bottom of the pile to save it. She put it in between two gray ones. Safe. Probably nobody would pick gray ones.

Then she went up and down the aisles. She started with the aisle by the window where Obie sat. She wanted him to get first choice.

He took a yellow one.

His best friend, Arthur, took a yellow one, too.

Other people took yellow ones, too, and brown ones and orange ones. And the red ones. But not the hidden red one. Mrs.

Henry had said red and yellow and orange and brown were fall colors.

Hardly anyone took a blue paper, and only Bobby Bork took a yucky gray one. But he didn't take it from the bottom of the pile.

Katie got to Amelia. Amelia took yellow.

"Yellow is like the sun," Amelia said.

"I like yellow, too," Katie said. "But I have a red one."

"Red's nice, too," Amelia said.

The last aisle was Tiffany's aisle. Katie held out the pile of papers.

Tiffany flipped through them. "I want red," she said.

"Yellow is like the sun," Katie said.

"I want red," Tiffany said.

Katie made her shoulders go up in a big shrug. "Brown is nice," Katie said. "It's a fall color."

Tiffany's bottom lip came out in a big pout. She looked as if she were going to cry.

Crybaby. Tiffany's a sniffle-snuffle crybaby, Katie thought. But she didn't say that out loud. She only said it inside her head where no one could hear.

"Orange is a good fall color!" Katie said out loud. "Black and orange for Halloween. Remember? Halloween's coming?"

Katie smiled.

Tiffany made a frowny face, and kept on looking through the papers.

When she got near the bottom, she said, "There! I see a red one!"

Katie pulled the papers back just a little. "I don't see any," she said.

"I do!" Tiffany said. "Right there! See!"

She grabbed Katie's hidden paper.

"That's mine!" Katie said.

"Not!" Tiffany said. "You have to choose last! That's the rule."

"I saved it!" Katie said.

"Mrs. Henry!" Tiffany called out. "Katie . . ."

"Hush up!" Katie said.

She could feel tears come to her eyes.

She blinked hard. She wasn't going to be a crybaby like Tiffany.

"What is it, Tiffany?" Mrs. Henry said. She looked up from helping Bobby with glue. She sounded a little mad.

"It's nothing," Katie said. She pulled out the red paper and plopped it on Tiffany's desk. "There!" she said. "You can have it!"

Tiffany smiled, kind of a mean smile.

"Say thank you," Katie said.

Tiffany didn't say thank you, though. She didn't say anything. She just began folding her red paper. She folded it over once and then over again.

Katie turned and went back to her seat.

When she sat down, she looked over at Tiffany, watched her folding her paper over *a third time*. It looked like she was making a card out of it. An invitation card.

Katie took a deep breath. Maybe, she thought. Maybe it's for me.

Halloween's Coming

But Tiffany didn't make an invitation. And by the time school was over that day, Katie knew why. Because Tiffany wasn't going to invite Katie to the party, that's why. Katie heard Tiffany tell Susan that she could invite only four friends for her party on Halloween night.

Katie counted. Tiffany had already invited Amelia. And Susan. And Jessica. And Mary.

That made four.

No party for Katie. And even worse, if Amelia went to the party, then Katie wouldn't have a best friend to go trick-or-treating with on Halloween night. There would be nobody but her brothers or Grandma or Grandpa. She pictured herself going up and down the street with Baby-Child, being bored, bored, bored. Baby-Child was going to be dressed up as a bunny. That was boring. Dumb, too, because bunnies weren't scary.

Halloween was going to be boring and dumb and sad.

When Katie got on the bus, she plopped down beside Amelia in the front seat. Obie was across the aisle in the other front seat with Arthur.

Katie and Amelia always sat in front, right behind Mr. Barker, the driver. They liked helping Mr. Barker drive, telling him where to stop and who got off where.

"Did you decide what you're going to be for Halloween?" Amelia asked when Katie sat down.

"I'm not going to be anything," Katie

said in her mad voice. "Just the sister of a dumb bunny."

"You mean you're going to be a bunny?" Amelia asked.

Katie rolled her eyes. "No!" she said. "Bunnies aren't for Halloween. They're for Easter. Halloween should be scary. I'm not going to be anything."

"I'm something," Amelia said. "I'm going to be a ballerina."

"At Tiffany's party?" Katie said.

Amelia nodded and looked away.

Katie sighed.

"What do you mean, you're not going to be anything?" Mr. Barker said over his shoulder. "Everybody has to dress up as something for Halloween."

"Do you dress up?" Katie asked him.

"Sure do," he said. He got the bus doors closed and the bus into gear and started up. "Every year I dress up as a school-bus driver."

He laughed as if he had said something funny.

18

"But you *are* a school-bus driver," Katie said.

Mr. Barker laughed again. "Yup. And I have a haunted house, too. Every year my wife and I make our house into a haunted house."

"A haunted house?" Katie said. She leaned forward. "How do you make a haunted house?"

"Oh," Mr. Barker said. "It's not hard. We set up a pretend coffin and a tombstone and invite ghosts to come over. And some witches. Sometimes I'm even a witch."

"You can't be a witch," Katie said.

"I am," Mr. Barker said.

"Can't be," Katie answered.

"Why not?" Mr. Barker asked.

"Because you're a boy," Amelia piped up.

"Boys can't be witches?" Mr. Barker asked.

"Nope," Katie said. "Boys have to be warlocks, right, Amelia?"

"Right," Amelia said. "They're boy witches."

"Oh," Mr. Barker said. "Then I'm a warlock."

"But there's really no such thing as witches and warlocks, right?" Obie said, leaning across the aisle. He sounded a little worried. "And no such thing as ghosts, either. Not real ones. Right?"

Katie made a face at her brother. " 'Course there's not real witches and ghosts," she said. "There are no such things."

"I knew that," Obie said.

"But some look real," Katie said. "I can look like a witch." She turned to Amelia and made her fingers into claws and pulled her lips up off her teeth. "See?" she said.

"That's a really good witch face," Amelia said. "It's scary."

"Thank you," Katie said.

She turned back to Mr. Barker. "How do you make a haunted house?" she asked. "Besides getting witches and ghosts to come.

And how do you make pretend coffins and stuff?"

"Oh," Mr. Barker said, "it's easy. Use whatever you have around the house. Like, we put on spooky music and get some candles and spiderwebs and . . ."

"Fake spiderwebs, right?" Obie asked.

Mr. Barker didn't answer. He was pulling up at the stop for Arthur and Bobby Bork.

He opened the bus doors.

Arthur got off, waving good-bye to Obie.

Bobby got off, too, holding his gray leaf paper. He waved to Mr. Barker when he went down the steps. Then he dropped his leaf paper.

Mr. Barker waited until Bobby picked up his paper, and then the bus moved away.

When the bus started up, Obie said again, "Fake spiderwebs, right, Mr. Barker?"

"Right," Mr. Barker said. "Fake spiderwebs."

"I knew that," Obie said.

But he sounded like he'd been a little worried.

Katie wasn't worried, though. She had begun to smile.

Because she had begun to have a thought. Make a plan.

Stupid crybaby Tiffany wasn't going to spoil her Halloween. Mom had said no party this year. But she hadn't said no anything else.

Katie's plan got bigger and bigger. And it was Mr. Barker who had given her the idea.

She couldn't wait to get off the bus and tell Obie.

4

Haunted House

"I have a plan," Katie said, as soon as she got off the bus with Obie. She swung her backpack round and round. "A good plan. For Halloween."

"Did Tiffany ask you?" Obie said. "To her party?"

"No," Katie said. "Tiffany's a crybaby. But guess what? I have a different plan."

Obie looked at Katie. "A haunted house!" Katie said.

"I'm going to have a haunted house just like Mr. Barker has."

"With witches and warlocks?" Obie said.

"Yep. And I'm going to invite everybody. Everybody except crybaby Tiffany."

"Good," Obie said. "She's mean."

"Want to help?" Katie said.

Obie nodded. "Where would we have it?"

"I don't know," Katie said. "Somewhere."

She swung her backpack some more, round and round in front of her. Her favorite tiny baby bear, Koala, slipped out of her backpack onto the ground. Koala was her lucky bear. He sat on the end of her pencil during spelling tests. And once, when there was a mean substitute teacher, Katie held Koala in the palm of her hand all day long. His soft fur made her feel better. He was so small that it was easy for him to fit inside her hand or on the end of a pencil — and to slide out of small openings.

Katie bent to pick him up. "Poor

Koala," she said. She dusted him off with one finger.

"Is he all right?" Obie asked.

Katie blew some dirt off his soft fur and put him in her pocket. "He's okay now," she said. "He didn't mind. Maybe he can come to the haunted house, too. Wherever we have it."

"We could have it in the basement," Obie said.

Katie smiled and fingered Koala. "Yeah!" she said. "It's dark and spooky. We can make it more spooky."

"Not too spooky," Obie said. He looked down at his sneakers. "It would scare Baby-Child," he said.

"Oh," Katie said. "But we wouldn't let him come anyway. He's too little."

"I think it will be hard to do," Obie asked. "And we'll need money. For fake spiderwebs and stuff."

Katie nodded. "I have money," she said. "A little. Two dollars, I think. About."

"I have sixteen dollars and forty-four cents," Obie said.

"You do?" Katie made her eyes get wide. "How come?"

"Allowance. I save it," Obie said. "And when Mom gives us money for the candy store, I only spend half."

"Oh," Katie said. "I never save. But Obie, who could help us? I mean, making a coffin and spooky stuff, that might be hard."

Obie made his frowny face. "Ask Sam?" he said. "Or Matthew?"

Katie shook her head. She didn't want her big brothers helping. They always took over. She chewed her lip. And she had a feeling she shouldn't ask Mom. Or Daddy. She was just a little worried. It wasn't a Halloween party. It wasn't a party at all. But still, she wondered if Mom would think it was too much like a party. Although Mom was going to be away, and Daddy, too. They might not even find out.

"Maybe we'll just do it ourselves," Katie said.

"Okay," Obie agreed.

They came up the hill and around the corner to their street. In their driveway, they could see a big blue car, and someone taking packages out of it.

Grandma! Even from all the way down the block, Katie recognized Grandma and the car.

"Grandma!" Katie said. "Grandpa!" She started to run.

Obie ran, too.

"Grandma, hi, Grandma!" Katie yelled.

Grandma turned to Katie, her arms out. "Run and I'll swing you!" Grandma called.

Katie ran fast, and threw herself into Grandma's arms.

Grandma lifted Katie up and spun her round and round.

Then Grandma set Katie down and put her arms out for Obie.

But Obie just wanted a hug. He didn't like swinging very much.

"Grandma!" Katie said, when she had caught her breath. "Where's Grandpa?

When's Mom and Daddy going away? Are you staying till Halloween?"

Grandma smiled. "When is that?"

"When is it?" Katie said. "This week!"

"Five days," Obie said. He looked at his watch. "Five days and . . . and some hours but I don't know how many."

Grandma smiled again. Grandma smiled lots. And she did lots of good things with Katie. Once, she and Grandpa even built a whole treehouse for Obie and Katie. Grandma always said that together, she and Grandpa could do practically anything.

Anything?

Katie smiled to herself. Maybe they could even help with the haunted house!

"Grandma!" she said. "Could you help me with something?"

Grandma smiled again. "I'm sure I could. But first you help me here."

She bent and pulled some more packages out of the car. She handed one to Katie and one to Obie, and took a big one herself. Obie's package smelled like cookies.

"What kind?" Katie said, bending and sniffing at Obie's package.

Grandma laughed. "What kind, what?" she said.

Katie laughed, too. She knew Grandma knew what she meant.

But Obie said, "What kind of cookies?"

"You'll have to ask Grandpa," Grandma said. "He baked them."

"Where is he?" Katie asked again.

"He's in the house," Grandma said. "Come on, I think we might have some presents for you and for Matthew and Sam and Baby-Child, too. Halloween presents, I think."

Katie looked at Obie, and they both smiled.

Then they followed Grandma to the house.

Presents, Katie thought, as she held tight to her box. Maybe, just maybe, her present was a witch costume. A great witch costume.

For the haunted house.

The haunted house that Grandma and Grandpa would help her make.

5

Grandpa's Here!

The only thing was, Katie's present was not a witch costume. It was not any kind of costume. It was a book, a Halloween book. Obie's present was a book, too, and from the look of the packages, Matthew's present was a book and Sam's present was a book. Even Baby-Child got a book.

Katie tried not to look disappointed. And she also couldn't help noticing that Baby-Child's book was bigger than hers.

"Thank you, Grandma," Katie said politely, when she opened her present. "Where's Grandpa?"

"Out here in the kitchen!" Grandpa called out.

Katie put her book up on the table, out of reach of Baby-Child, who was crawling around the living room, and hurried to the kitchen.

Grandpa was sitting at the table with Katie's big brothers, Matthew and Sam, and Mom. Grandpa's leg was up on a chair in front of him. His foot was all wrapped up in a big white cast, and there were crutches next to him.

"What happened?" Katie asked.

Grandpa reached for Katie and pulled her close. He kissed her hair and hugged her.

She hugged him back. "Huh?" she said. "What'd you do to it?"

"Broke my ankle," he said. "I fell when I was running."

"Does it hurt?" Katie said. "Can I try your crutches?"

"They're too big for you," Matthew said.

"Way too big," Sam said. "For a shrimp."

Katie made a face at her brothers.

"Be nice, Katie!" Mom said.

Katie rolled her eyes. She turned back to Grandpa. "Can I try them?" she asked. "Please?"

Grandpa smiled. "You can try."

"Now don't fall and hurt yourself," Grandma said. She came into the room with Baby-Child in her arms. Obie came with her, still holding the box that smelled like cookies.

Katie tucked one crutch under one arm and one under the other and tried to walk to Grandma. It was hard to do. She moved one crutch and then the other, and then swung herself forward. One crutch slipped out from under her arm, and she fell.

"Told you!" Matthew said.

"You're way too little for them!" Sam said.

"Be nice!" Mom said. "Are you all right, Katie?"

Katie nodded and picked herself up.

She went to Grandma and lifted the lid off the box. It was oatmeal cookies!

"Grandpa!" Katie said, turning to him. "How did you make cookies if your leg is broken?"

"It wasn't too hard," Grandpa said. "I did all the work sitting down. Then Grandma put them in the oven for me."

"Do you have to keep sitting down?" Katie asked.

Grandpa sighed. "For two whole weeks."

Two weeks. Halloween would be over in just five days. And it would be too late for Grandpa to help with the haunted house.

Katie looked at Grandma.

"And I have to keep watch over him every minute," Grandma said. "He's like a big baby. He'd go out running again if I didn't watch him."

"Would you really, Grandpa?" Katie said.

Grandpa shook his head. "Not really," he said. "Your grandma exaggerates."

"What does that mean?" Katie said.

"It means she says more than is true," Obie said. "Right, Grandpa?"

"Right," Grandpa said. "Because I wouldn't go out running." He winked at Katie. "But I might walk if I could get away from Grandma," he said softly. "I keep sending her these thoughts. 'Go away!' I say in my thoughts. But she doesn't go."

Grandma laughed and shook her head. "See what I mean?" she said. "I have to keep an eye on him. And it will take more than thoughts to get rid of me."

Katie looked from Grandma to Grandpa to Mom. Mom was putting coffee into the coffeepot.

Ask Mom?

She sighed. No.

Katie picked up her books and went up to her room. She didn't know how, but she knew she'd figure it out. One way or another, she'd have a great haunted house. And stupid crybaby Tiffany wasn't going to come.

6

No Monsters

That night, Katie tiptoed into Obie's room. She was supposed to be in bed, but she couldn't sleep. All she could think about was Halloween and the haunted house — think about *and* worry about. Also, Mom and Dad were leaving the next day. And even though Katie liked having Grandpa and Grandma there, still, she always felt a little worried in her stomach the night before Mom and Daddy left.

"Obie!" she whispered. "Obie, wake up!" She bent over his bed.

Obie was buried under his covers, head

and all. "Obie!" she whispered again. She tugged on the covers.

"Go away!" Obie said. "I'm not here!"

Katie pulled on the covers some more. "You are too here!" she said.

Obie sat up. "Oh," he said. "It's you." He pulled his knees up and wrapped his arms around them.

Katie sat down on the bed. "Who did you think it was?" she said.

Obie didn't answer for a minute. Then he said, "A monster. And don't laugh."

Katie didn't laugh.

"How come you thought it was a monster?" she said.

"Because sometimes I think a monster lives under my bed," Obie said. "But if I hide under the covers, he can't get me. And don't laugh!"

"I'm not laughing," Katie said. "Know what?"

"What?" Obie said.

"Sometimes a monster lives in my closet," Katie said in a whispery voice. "Especially when Mom and Daddy go away."

"It does?" Obie said.

Katie nodded. "Sometimes. I can't get to sleep unless the closet door is closed tight. Grandma sometimes forgets to close it, though, and I have to get up and do it."

"I can't go to sleep unless the covers are over my head," Obie said. "Even when Mom and Daddy are here."

They were both quiet for a while.

"But there's no such thing as monsters, right?" Katie said.

"Right," Obie said. "But I get scared anyway sometimes. Especially at night."

"Me, too," Katie said. "Obie?"

"What?"

"What are we going to do about our haunted house?" Katie said. "Grandpa can't help. And Grandma can't, either. And you heard what Mom and Dad said at dinner."

"I know," Obie said. "They don't want Halloween kids here this year. Too much work for Grandma and Grandpa."

Katie nodded. Obie was right. At dinner, Mom and Dad were telling Grandma and Grandpa about other Halloweens. Daddy told about the time Obie was dressed like a mummy and his entire suit unwrapped just as he was about to go trick-or-treating. And then after Mom and Dad got him wound up again, he had to go to the bathroom and so they had to unwind him and then afterwards wind him back up all over again.

And the time at the party last year when six girls came and they were all dressed exactly alike as ballerinas, and four of them cried and wanted to go home and change their costumes into something else.

And the year it rained and the paper costumes all dissolved.

Dad said no ghosts or ballerinas or mummies underfoot this year. And Mom said so, too. "You'll have your hands full as it is," Mom had said to Grandma.

"So what do we do?" Obie said.

"I was thinking something," Katie said. "What if we had our haunted house in the shed out back — you know, where Daddy keeps his tools and the lawn mower? Think that would be all right?"

"I think they'd still say no," Obie said.

"But they wouldn't have to know," Katie said. "Not until Halloween night. And by then, it would be too late to say no."

"But when they find out, they'll get mad," Obie said.

Katie shook her head. "Grandma never gets mad. Besides, it won't be any trouble for them. See, if it's just in the shed, it's not like the basement and so people won't be underfoot like Daddy said. I mean, it's far back behind the garage. Nobody even sees it, except Daddy when he goes back there for the lawn mower. We can just put up spiderwebs and . . ."

"Fake ones, right?" Obie said.

"Right," Katie said. "And maybe some candles to make it spooky. And you know my toy chest? We could make believe it's a coffin like Mr. Barker said, and have a ghost in it and . . ."

"A fake one, right?" Obie said.

"Right," Katie said. "Or a dead body. A fake dead body," she added, before Obie could say it.

"What about candy and soda? You can't have a party without candy and soda," Obie said.

"This isn't a party," Katie said.

"You still need candy and soda. Or cupcakes," Obie said. "Or something."

Katie sighed. But then she had a thought. "I know what!" she said. "Grandpa can make us cookies! Even with his broken ankle, he can bake cookies. Isn't that a good idea?"

"It is a good idea," Obie said. "Now can I go back to sleep?"

"Okay," Katie said.

She tiptoed out of his room. But at the door, she turned and looked back.

Even in the dark, she could tell that Obie was buried under his covers again.

"Obie?" she said.

"What?"

His voice came out all muffled.

"Remember?" she said. "There's no such thing as monsters."

"I remember," Obie answered. But he still stayed under the covers.

The List

Early the next morning, Mom and Dad said good-bye to Katie and Obie. They'd be at their convention for five whole days, until the day after Halloween.

"Now, have fun," Mom said as she kissed Katie. "And remember to stay close to Grandma on Halloween when you go trick-or-treating. Grandma's going to make you your witch costume today."

"I might not go trick-or-treating," Katie said.

Mom looked surprised. "Why?" she asked.

Katie just shrugged. She couldn't tell about the haunted house.

"Well," Dad said. "You'll have fun whatever you do. Just remember, no parties or anything like that. Grandma and Grandpa are going to have enough to do."

Katie felt a little worried all over again. Was a haunted house too much like a party?

She felt a little sad, too, when Mom and Dad pulled out of the driveway and waved good-bye. But after they left, she wasn't as sad, because she had some things to look forward to. Like, today she'd make her invitation list. And Grandma and Grandpa had promised everybody a treat for that night. They'd go to McDonald's, the new one where they had the indoor playground with the mazes. And where you could buy Happy Meals, Happy Pizza Meals.

Later, at school, during free time, Katie started on her invitation list. She was going to write down the names of every boy and every girl in the entire class. All except crybaby Tiffany. Then, after school, she was going to go home and make invitations, and the following day, she'd hand them out. Maybe on the playground after school. Or maybe on the bus. That way, it wouldn't really be school, so she wouldn't have to give one to Tiffany.

Katie was halfway through her list when Mrs. Henry said, "Free time is over now. Take out your math workbooks, please. Today is add and take away."

Katie put the list in her desk and took out her math workbook. She looked over at Amelia. "Easy," she whispered. "Add and take away is easy."

Amelia nodded. "Except for take away," she said.

"I'll help you," Katie said.

"Are you paying attention, Katie?" Mrs. Henry said.

Katie felt her ears get hot.

"Yes," she said.

"Good," Mrs. Henry said, and she smiled at Katie.

That was what Katie liked about Mrs. Henry. She didn't stay mad.

Mrs. Henry wrote two page numbers on the board.

Katie turned to the pages in her workbook. "Easy!" she whispered to herself. Even take away was easy for Katie. A lot easier than spelling. Katie hated spelling.

She picked up her pencil and finished the whole two pages in about a minute.

She looked around the room.

Everyone else was working, and some people were frowning and chewing on their pencils. Not Obie, though. Obie was smiling. He was super good at math, too. He was also good at spelling.

At the desk next to Katie, Amelia was frowning hard. Katie knew it was about the take away. And on the other side of her, Tiffany was carefully smoothing her paper, erasing little tiny dust smudges and brushing the eraser dust away with her hand.

Katie leaned out of her seat toward Tiffany. "I'm already finished," she whispered.

Tiffany raised her hand. "Mrs. Henry!" she said.

Mrs. Henry didn't look up. "Later, please, Tiffany," Mrs. Henry said. "Just do your work."

"But Mrs. Henry!" Tiffany said. "Katie's bothering me."

Mrs. Henry looked up and frowned at Katie. "Katie?" she said. "Why aren't you doing your work?"

Katie felt her ears get hot again.

"I did do my work!" she said. "I'm already finished."

"You can't be finished already," Mrs. Henry said. "Go back and check your work, please."

Katie sighed.

Checking work was dumb. If you just did the work, what good was checking it? How were you going to tell if it was wrong just a teensy-weensy minute later?

But she bent her head and pretended to check her work. Instead, though, she slid the invitation list out of her desk.

She put it inside the workbook and bent over it. She already had half the boys — Arthur and Oscar and Bobby Bork and Simon James. Oh, and Obie! She couldn't forget Obie.

And she had Susan and Amelia, and . . .

But then she remembered. Amelia couldn't come — not if she was going to Tiffany's party.

She looked over at Amelia. Amelia was still frowning at her take-aways, bending her fingers one by one and counting them.

Katie leaned over and peeked at Amelia's paper. Half of the take-aways were wrong.

Katie looked around. Mrs. Henry was bent over her desk, doing something in the plan book.

Katie poked Amelia. "The first answer is eleven," she whispered.

Amelia nodded and erased her answer. She wrote in the number eleven.

"And number three should be seven," Katie whispered.

Amelia didn't look over at Katie. But she erased her number three answer and put in the number seven.

Katie made a quick look up at Mrs. Henry. She was still busy with her plan book.

"Want to come to my haunted house on Halloween?" Katie whispered. "And fix number seven. It's fourteen. That one was hard."

Amelia erased her number seven answer. But the paper got all wrinkled up and she had to smooth it out, and there were dirty smudges of pencil and eraser marks all over it.

She rolled her eyes at Katie.

"It's all right," Katie whispered.

"Mrs. Henry!"

It was Tiffany again. "Mrs. Henry, Katie's not doing her own work," she called out.

Mrs. Henry looked up.

She made a mad frown at Katie.

Katie felt herself get scared. She didn't

want to be in trouble. Anyway, helping her friend wasn't bad. Not really.

"I'm doing my own work," Katie said. "I did it a long time ago."

Mrs. Henry just sighed. "I hope you get a hundred percent, Katie," she said. "And I don't want to have to speak to you again."

She went back to her plan book.

Katie turned and made a witch face at Tiffany.

Then she looked up and down the rows, counting every single person. Seventeen. She checked her list. Sixteen names there. Sixteen names, because she hadn't counted Tiffany. Sixteen people invited to her haunted house.

But then she had a bad worry thought: Could sixteen people fit in the shed? Could sixteen people fit, especially if there was a coffin and a witch and spiderwebs all over the place? And then she had another worry thought: What about snacks? Even if

Grandpa made cookies, would he make enough? And what would she tell Grandma and Grandpa about wanting to take the cookies out to the shed?

It was a problem. A really big problem. She looked across the room at Obie. He was finished with add and take away, too. He was making little wiggly waves with his pencil in the air, like he was flying a make-believe plane.

He saw Katie looking, and he smiled and wiggled his pencil plane at her. She smiled back and wiggled her pencil back. Maybe the haunted house wasn't such a big problem. She and Obie, they were like Grandma and Grandpa. Together, they could do practically anything.

8

New Invitations

After school that day, Katie and Obie made up the haunted house invitations. Katie did hers in her room, and Obie did his in his room. They were going to get together after and compare. Obie was doing the boys. Katie was doing the girls. Minus Tiffany. Take away Tiffany. Katie laughed out loud. She knew that would make Amelia laugh, too. But Amelia was still a problem. Would she come to the haunted house? Instead of Tiffany's party? Maybe she would, if everyone else was coming.

Katie sat down at her desk. She took

out black construction paper and a red marker. Red was good for making drippy blood. She made a picture of a monster with red, squiggly lines on its face. The only thing was, the red didn't show up on black. But then Katie found a way. She colored over and over and over on the same spot. It came out very red. But the paper got kind of thin, too.

Oh, well. It was red. And drippy. Like blood. A red, red monster.

When she was all finished with the

monster and with the red squiggly lines, she wrote down the words:

Come to are Hunted Hous.
It will be scarey.
Reel monsters and dead peeple.
Cookies surved.

She took the invitation to Obie's room. He was working on his computer.

"You're supposed to be doing invitations," Katie said.

Obie turned. "I am," he said. "I already did them. See?"

He held up a piece of paper. It was white paper with red and black designs all over it, very fancy, done with the computer and color printer. It was folded in half and then in half again, like a real invitation. The only thing was, the designs were of airplanes — airplanes with blood dripping from them.

"See?" he said. "Like it?"

"Airplanes?" Katie said. "Why airplanes?"

Obie shrugged. "I like them," he said.

"Oh," Katie said.

"Read it," Obie said. He held it out to her.

Katie took it and read:

Come to our Haunted House!
Halloween Night! After dark!
Refreshments served.

"Wow!" Katie said. "It looks real, like it came from a store. And I like that word *refreshments*. That's what Mrs. Henry always says about parties, that we should bring refreshments."

"Thank you," said Obie. "Let's see yours."

Katie looked at her invitation. The paper was thin and kind of holey from where she had worked extra hard with the red Magic Marker. She noticed too that the spelling was different from Obie's. She would bet that Obie's was right and hers was wrong.

She put hers behind her back.

"It's not finished yet," she said.

"Can I see anyway?" Obie said.

Katie scrunched up her face and shook her head. "It's not very good. Obie, would you make mine, too? For the girls? Just like yours, only not with planes?"

"I bet yours is good, too," Obie said.

"Not that good," Katie said.

"What do you want instead of planes?" Obie said.

"Monsters," Katie said.

"Okay," Obie said.

He went back to the computer.

After just a few minutes, he had a whole drawing done. He pushed the printer button and the new ones came out — with the same words as his, only with drippy red monsters on them.

"These are cool!" Katie said. She smiled at her brother. "Know what this means? It means we're really, truly going to have a haunted house."

"I knew that," Obie said. And then he said, "Katie, should we invite Sam and Matt?"

"No way!" Katie said. "They'll take over."

Obie just shrugged. "Not if we have it all done first," he said. "We could just invite them to come see."

"They're too bossy," Katie said. "Come on, Obie. Let's set things up in the shed. Help me move my toy box."

"What if Grandma sees us taking it out?" Obie said.

"She won't," Katie said.

"You mean you hope she won't," Obie said.

Katie nodded. "That's what I mean," she said.

Koala's Lost

Grandma didn't see. She was busy with Baby-Child when they carried the toy box downstairs and outside. Also, the shed was hidden behind the garage, so no one could see unless they came looking back there. And why would anybody do that? The only person who went there was Daddy, because he kept the lawn mower and leaf blower there. And Daddy wasn't even around.

Katie and Obie worked very hard. First, they moved the lawn mower out of the shed and parked it around back. That was very hard to do, especially when it tipped and almost squashed Katie's toes. Then they took Katie's toy box and set it in one corner of the shed. They put a chair in another corner for a witch to sit on. That was for Katie. Grandma had made her a wonderful witch costume, with a big cape and a pointy black hat. They put Obie's little play table that he'd had since he was a baby in the middle of the shed. That was for the refreshments. And then Katie took candles and candle holders out of the dining room and brought them to the shed, too. She took every single candle and candle holder she could find. She thought of bringing matches but decided that might be a bad thing to do. Even though they'd have to light the candles sometime, she didn't need to figure it out yet.

Anyway, by then it was almost dark and they could hear Grandma calling them to dinner. And then, after dinner, it was time for homework and for playing some games with Grandpa, so they had to put off any more work on the haunted house till next day.

The next day was also hand-out-invitations day. Katie and Obie had decided they'd do it after school. They'd do it out on the sidewalk where the walkers passed by and where the buses got loaded up. That way, it wasn't *in* school, and they could give invitations to the kids who didn't ride the bus and also the ones who did.

All day in school, Katie kept looking at the invitations inside her backpack. They were perfect, just like store-bought ones. She was looking at them when Mrs. Henry said it was time for spelling.

"Take everything off your desks now," Mrs. Henry said. "Time for this week's spelling test."

There was a lot of noise while people dumped stuff inside their desks.

Katie slid her backpack under her desk. She took a last quick look at the spelling list when she put her book away. *Wish* was the first word, W-I-S-H. Katie whispered it over and over to herself. I *wish* we didn't have a spelling test each week. I *wish* I had studied my spelling words.

Every week, she went over the words with Mom. But Mom wasn't there last night, and Katie had forgotten to ask Grandma. Well, she'd sort of forgotten. She also sort of hadn't wanted to remember. But now she wished she had.

W-I-S-H, *wish*, she said to herself.

"Get out paper and pencil now," Mrs. Henry said. "Does anyone need to sharpen pencils first?"

"I do!" Obie said. He and a bunch of other people jumped up. Obie went up to the pencil sharpener and sharpened two pencils. Obie had a desk full of sharpened pencils.

When everyone sat back down, Mrs. Henry said, "All right? Is everybody ready now?"

A bunch of people said, "Ready."

Katie sighed. She wasn't ready. She was never ready for spelling. Not even when she studied. But then she remembered Koala. Lucky Koala. He would help.

She bent to her backpack and reached for baby Koala. Koala had helped her lots of times before.

She dug around inside her backpack. No Koala.

"Are you ready, Katie?" Mrs. Henry said. "Sit up straight and tall now."

Katie sat up straight and tall. But she kept worrying. Where was Koala?

"First word," Mrs. Henry said. "First word is *spider*."

Easy, Katie thought.

She wrote it down. S-P-I-D-U-R.

She frowned at it. It looked funny.

Maybe it was S-P-I-D-I-R?

She slid a little sideways in her seat and reached under the desk again. Koala. She needed Koala.

"Next word," Mrs. Henry said. "Next word is . . . Katie, are you paying attention?"

Katie straightened up. She felt her ears get hot.

"I'm paying attention," she said.

"Good," Mrs. Henry said. "Next word is *nickel*."

Katie thought.

N-I-K-E-L?

She slid a sideways look at Tiffany. Tiffany was very good at spelling. She was writing with one hand, and the other was curled around her paper, like she was shading it from the sun.

Katie reached under her desk again. Koala. She remembered putting him in her backpack the other day. She remembered him falling out. But she also remembered picking him up and blowing the dust off him and putting him back. But what if he had fallen out again and she hadn't seen him?

She could feel tears come to her eyes. She felt and felt inside her backpack. No Koala.

"*Wish*," Mrs. Henry said. "The next word is *wish*."

Katie straightened up and took a deep breath. Easy.

W-I-S-H.

She smiled. She was practically sure that was right.

"And the next word," Mrs. Henry said, "the next word is *orange*." She said it again. "*Orange*."

Katie chewed on her lip. O-R-E-N-G. No. Maybe it was O-R-I-N-G-E?

Mrs. Henry sneezed. She turned to her desk for a tissue.

Katie quickly dove under her desk. She grabbed the backpack and dumped it over.

The invitations fell out. So did Katie's old crayons. So did about a million other things. They made a lot of noise.

Katie straightened up. She felt herself getting very scared.

"What was that?" Mrs. Henry said. She looked all around the room.

Nobody said anything.

Nobody but Tiffany. "It was Katie," Tiffany said. "She's cheating. She's trying to get her speller out of her backpack to peek."

"I am not!" Katie burst out. "I'm trying to find Koala. He's lost." She could feel tears come to her eyes.

"Katie!" Mrs. Henry said. "Why are you looking for a toy when we're having a spelling test? Come up and sit here till the spelling test is over." She pointed to the time-out chair. "Bring your paper with you," she added.

"I'm not cheating!" Katie said. "And I wasn't looking in my speller."

"I know that," Mrs. Henry said kindly. "But come up here anyway."

Katie didn't get up. She folded her arms. She was not going to sit in the time-out chair. Only bad kids sat in the time-out chair. "Tiffany took my Koala!" Katie said, upset.

"Me?" Tiffany said. "I did not!"

Mrs. Henry looked at Tiffany. "Did you, Tiffany?" she asked.

"No!" Tiffany said.

"Are you sure you didn't pick it up by

SPELLING TEST

mistake, Tiffany?" Mrs. Henry said.

"No, I didn't!" Tiffany sounded like she was going to cry. "I don't want that dirty old thing!"

"He's not dirty!" Katie said.

Mrs. Henry sighed. "All right," she said. "That's enough of this. We'll discuss it later, both of you. You can stay at your desk for now, Katie. But I want to see both of you at recess time."

Katie took a deep breath.

At least she didn't have to sit in the time-out chair.

Mrs. Henry gave the next word.

"*Equal*," she said. "The next word is *equal*."

Katie bent over her paper.

E-K-W-E-L, she wrote.

She didn't dare dig for Koala or even stuff things back into her backpack.

But while she waited for the next word, she did look down at the invitations lying on the floor. She smiled. None of them were for Tiffany.

Tiffany was mean. Tiffany lied. Tiffany tried to get Katie in trouble.

But Katie also knew that Tiffany probably hadn't taken her Koala, either.

For just a little minute, Katie felt sort of bad.

10

No Recess

Katie had to stay in at recess, and so did Tiffany. But Mrs. Henry wasn't really mad. She just made each of them clean out their desks and look for Koala and throw away any trash they found. Then they cleaned out their backpacks, and their cubbies, too. They looked all over for Koala. They didn't find him anywhere. But Katie did find a lot of junk.

Tiffany didn't have any junk. Her desk was perfect. Perfect Tiffany.

Perfectly mean Tiffany.

"No more fighting, girls, all right?"

Mrs. Henry said when they were all finished and Katie had thrown away all her trash. "And this was such a good idea," Mrs. Henry added, "that I think I'll have all the boys and girls clean their desks out when they get back in from recess."

And that's what she did. Mrs. Henry made everyone clean out their desks. She told them to look for Koala, too, just in case someone had picked him up by accident.

Mrs. Henry marked the spelling papers while the class did their cleanup.

People kept going to the front of the room to the trash basket. Bobby Bork made about a thousand trips. "How could he have that much junk in one little desk?" Katie said to Amelia.

"Maybe he's practicing to be a garbage man when he grows up," Amelia said.

"Maybe he's practicing to be a magician," Katie said. "Fitting all that stuff in one tiny place."

Amelia laughed.

Katie took a load of junk from Amelia

and carried it to the basket for her.

"Know what?" Katie said when she came back. "I saw a whole sandwich in the trash. It smelled like sardines. I bet it was Bobby's. And there was a smushed-up airplane, too. I was going to take it for Obie, but it was wet. I think the sandwich leaked on it."

"Does Obie like planes?" Amelia said.

"Not wet ones," Katie said.

She looked across the room at Obie. He was reading a book, one hand on either side of his head, pressing his ears in. He was allowed to read because he didn't have to clean out his desk. His was perfectly clean.

Katie made a frowny face. Obie was a little bit like Tiffany, she thought — perfect. Even his ears, though he didn't think so. She wished he wouldn't worry about them so much. They were really very nice ears.

Mrs. Henry was finished marking the spelling papers.

She started walking up and down the aisles, handing the papers back.

First she did Tiffany's aisle.

Then she did Katie's aisle. Katie squinched her eyes closed when Mrs. Henry got close. She opened them when Mrs. Henry put her paper down on the desk in front of her. The paper was all marked up. In red.

One word was right. Nine words were wrong.

The only one right was W-I-S-H.

"Did you study, Katie?" Mrs. Henry asked.

Katie nodded, but she didn't look up.

She wished Mom hadn't gone away.

"You know you have to write each wrong word ten times tonight, Katie," Mrs. Henry said. "That's the rule, remember? And say them out loud when you write them. It will help."

Katie nodded, but she sighed. She'd write them ten times. It wouldn't help, though. She could write them a thousand times, and say them out loud a thousand times, and she'd still get them wrong.

She looked over at perfect Tiffany.

Tiffany had left her paper on the corner of her desk. One hundred percent. Tiffany didn't have a single one wrong.

Tiffany was reading a Halloween book that she'd gotten from the library.

It had a scary-looking witch on the cover, but Tiffany was smiling as she read.

Actually, Katie thought, Tiffany was kind of pretty when she smiled. She had a dimple in her cheek.

Katie pressed a finger into her own cheek. She wondered if she could make a dimple if she kept her finger there long enough. And how long would be long enough?

Tiffany looked up and saw Katie watching her.

Katie smiled at Tiffany. She wanted to make up. She had made Tiffany lose recess time. And she didn't really think Tiffany had taken Koala.

But Tiffany didn't smile back. She made a mad face at Katie, practically a witch face.

"I was thinking something nice about you," Katie said. "But now I'm not."

"You were not thinking something nice," Tiffany said.

"Was too!" Katie said.

"What?" Tiffany said.

"I'm not telling now!" Katie said.

"See? Told you!" Tiffany said.

Katie made a mad face back. "You have a dent in your cheek," she said. "A dumb hole."

"It's not a dent and it's not a hole. It's a dimple!" Tiffany said.

"Is too a dent," Katie said. "Dumb, dumb, dumb." She spelled it out. "D-U-M-B, dumb," she said.

"That's the only word you know how to spell!" Tiffany said.

"Is not," Katie said.

"Bet!" Tiffany said.

She pointed to Katie's spelling paper. Katie looked down at her desk.

She felt her face get hot. Who cares? she said to herself. But she crumpled up the spelling paper and hid it inside her desk.

Jack-o'-lanterns

After school, Katie and Obie handed out their invitations at the bus port. They handed them out to the busers and the walkers. They handed them out to everybody but Tiffany.

Sixteen invitations.

Sixteen people invited to a haunted house. As soon as people read them, everybody said they wanted to come. Even Amelia said she'd come. She'd come before she went to crybaby Tiffany's party, she said.

Tiffany said she didn't care if she

wasn't invited. She said she wouldn't come anyway.

When Katie and Obie got off the bus, they hurried home to work on the haunted house. Katie stuck her hands in her pockets because it was cold. And that was when she discovered Koala. So that's where she had put him the other day!

She felt a little bad then for blaming Tiffany. And not inviting her to the party. But it was Tiffany's fault, that's all, and she didn't have any time to worry about Tiffany. Now that people had said they'd come, they really needed to work. Halloween was in just three more days. All they had set up so far was the table and the toy chest. They hadn't done anything about ghosts or spiderwebs or anything like that.

But when they got home, Grandma and Grandpa were waiting in the kitchen with their coats on. Grandma was holding Baby-Child. Baby-Child was wearing his white coat with the little ears on the hood. It made him look like a little baby rabbit.

"How about we go pick pumpkins?" Grandpa said. "The farm up the road is open. I saw it today. You pick a pumpkin, and if you guess the weight correctly, the pumpkin is yours free."

Pumpkins! Jack-o'-lanterns! Just what they needed for their haunted house. A scary pumpkin with a candle inside.

"But, Grandpa," Katie said. "You can't pick pumpkins with a broken leg." She turned to Grandma. "Can he? Will you let him?"

Grandma laughed. "He can't pick them," she said. "But I bet he can guess the pumpkin's weight and get it right."

"Can I get my own pumpkin?" Katie asked. "Do I get to guess the weight?"

"Me too?" Obie asked.

"Of course," Grandpa said. "Everyone gets his own pumpkin. We'll get one for Sam and one for Matthew, too. They're at scouts this afternoon."

"Can Baby-Child get one, too?" Obie said. He reached up and tickled Baby-Child's foot.

Baby-Child squealed and wiggled in Grandma's arms.

"A little one for Baby-Child," Grandma said.

They all piled into the car and put on seat belts and headed for the pumpkin place.

Katie and Obie picked out pumpkins for Sam and Matthew. Then they picked out pumpkins for themselves.

Katie picked herself a very round pumpkin. It was shaped like Baby-Child's head. Katie guessed it weighed five pounds and six ounces. But when the pumpkin man put it on the scale, he said it weighed nine pounds and two ounces.

Obie got a smaller pumpkin. His was funny-shaped, like a cigar. He said it weighed six pounds and fourteen ounces.

The pumpkin man weighed it. It weighed six pounds and fifteen ounces. But

Obie was so close, the man gave it to him free anyway.

Grandpa guessed close, but not close enough to get his free.

When they got home and Matthew and Sam got back from scouts, they all sat around the kitchen table and Grandpa helped them all carve the jack-o'-lanterns. All but Baby-Child. Grandma put him in his high chair to feed him.

Katie hated the way the pumpkin guts smelled when they cut inside. But Obie said it smelled good.

"Mine's the best!" Sam said after a while. He held up a very scary-looking pumpkin, with a mad frown on its face.

"Look at mine!" Matthew said. "Mine's more scary."

But Katie didn't think Matthew's was scary. She thought his was funny, with a big wide grin and some funny, crooked teeth.

"Can we put candles inside?" Sam asked Grandpa.

"Yes," Grandpa said. "If you promise

something — that you'll only light the candles when I'm around. A deal?"

"A deal," Matt and Sam said together.

Sam went off to the dining room to get the candles.

Uh-oh, Katie thought.

She had taken every single candle out to the shed. She had taken all the ones in the cabinet. She had taken all the candles on the sideboard. She had taken the white ones that were in the big silver candle holders on the table. And she had taken the silver candle holders, too.

Katie looked at Obie, but he wasn't looking back.

She could feel her heart beating hard. A scared feeling came into her stomach.

Sam came back into the kitchen. "There aren't any candles!" he said. "Where'd all the candles go?"

"They were there the other day," Grandma said. She turned away from the high chair and Baby-Child and looked at Sam. "Are you sure they're not there?"

"I'm sure," Sam said. "They're gone."

"That's funny," Grandma said.

She handed Baby-Child a spoon to bang on the high chair tray with, and went in the dining room with Sam.

Katie snuck a look at Obie.

She could feel her face getting hot.

Obie looked hot, too.

After a minute, Grandma and Sam came back into the kitchen. Without candles.

"I don't understand," Grandma said, looking at Grandpa. "There were a whole lot of candles on the sideboard and the table the other day."

Grandpa just shrugged.

"Do you kids have any ideas where your mom would have put the candles?" Grandma asked.

Katie bent over her pumpkin. She pretended to fix its lid. "Maybe Mom took them with her," she said.

"That's silly, Katie," Matthew said.

"Now why would your mom do that?" Grandma said.

Katie shrugged. "Maybe because she was afraid the power would go out," she said.

"Yeah," Obie said. "It does that sometimes. Like in that storm last summer."

"In a hotel?" Sam said.

"Hotels get storms, too," Katie said. "All the time, I bet."

"I don't think so, Katie," Grandma said. "I mean, hotels do have power outages. But I don't think Mom would take the candles with her, do you?"

"Actually, I do," Katie said, nodding. "I think so."

She snuck a look at Obie.

"Me, too," he said. "I think so, too."

And Katie crossed all her fingers. And hoped Grandma and Grandpa would think so, too.

Super Spooky Stuff

The next day, Katie and Obie worked super hard. They worked from the minute they got off the bus until it was too dark out to see anymore. They told Grandma and Grandpa that they were in their treehouse. Actually, they were in the shed.

First, though, they had to go to the store. Katie called it a candy store, but Grandma still called it a five-and-ten. It was right around the corner, a medium-sized store with things like candy and cards and batteries. And Halloween decorations. Katie and Obie were allowed to go there once a

AISLE 5

HALLOWE

costume
decoratio
masks

week to spend their allowance. This was the first time they'd gone there this week.

Katie took all the money she had — one dollar and ninety-seven cents. Obie took all his money — sixteen dollars and forty-four cents.

They bought lots of things that were super spooky. They got fake spiderwebs to string across the door and windows. They got a skeleton that was strung together with wire so that all the parts hung loose and wiggled. They got a black plastic cat, a big one with long yellow teeth. And they got a plastic skull whose jaw hung loose on a spring. When you moved the skull, the jaw jiggled, like the skull was talking to you. Obie got a big black plastic claw with fake blood on it, plastic fangs with fake blood, and a wig. But best of all, they got a flashlight. Bobby Bork had showed Obie a great trick. You had to be in a dark place. Then you held the flashlight under your chin and let the light shine up on your face. It made you look like a dead man, Bobby said.

When Katie and Obie got back to the shed, they started putting up all the stuff. Katie started with the spiderwebs and Obie took the skeleton.

"Look at me," Katie said after a minute. "Guess what I am." She turned to Obie, a long spiderweb draped all over her face.

"You look like a spider," Obie said.

"No," Katie said. "Guess."

"I did!" Obie said. He was walking around the shed, trying to find a place to hang the skeleton.

"Guess again!" Katie said.

"I told you, a spider," Obie said.

"Nope," Katie said.

She made humming, buzzing sounds to help Obie. She even flapped her arms a little.

Obie looked at her again and shrugged. "Beats me," he said.

"A fly!" Katie said. "Can't you tell? A fly in a spiderweb." She pretended again to flap her wing arms to try to get out.

"Oh," Obie said.

"I don't think I'd like to be a fly," Katie

said. She flung the web off her face and climbed up on the table. She strung the web across the window, hooking it from one side to the other. It was easy because the wood was all rough and the web just hung on it.

"Me neither," Obie said. "But I wouldn't want to be a spider either."

"If you had to be one or the other, what would you be?" Katie said.

Obie found a nail up by the ceiling and hung the skeleton on it. He stood back and looked at it. "There you go, Skelly," he said.

Katie stood back and looked at her spiderwebs. Pretty scary.

"I guess a spider, if I had to," Obie said.

"Me too," Katie said.

She put the black cat on the windowsill facing her. Then turned it around so it was facing out.

She went outside and looked at it. Very good. Very scary.

When she came back in, Obie was putting on his fangs. He put the black stringy wig on his head. Then he put on the fake bloody claw.

"Watch me!" he said. He climbed into the toy box, the toy box that was now a coffin. "I'm going to practice," he said. "But don't close the lid, okay?"

"Okay," Katie said.

She stood and watched while Obie settled himself in the box. He lay down, his knees pulled up because the box was kind of small. Then he closed his eyes. He folded his hands on his chest, the big black claw on top. His bloody fangs were hanging out of his mouth, and the wig was hanging over one eye. He lay there very still. Then, slowly, he began to sit up, groaning and making scary sounds.

Katie stepped back.

"Obie!" she said.

He stuck a claw out at her.

"Obie!" she said again. She backed up even more.

"What?" Obie said.

"Stop it!" she said.

Obie opened his eyes. "I was just pretending," he said.

"I know," Katie said. She hugged her arms to herself. "But you kind of scared me."

"I didn't mean to," Obie said. "But that means we'll scare everybody. I bet I'll scare Sam and Matt, too."

"We're not inviting them, remember?" Katie said.

"I know," Obie said. "I was just thinking."

"What about the refreshments?" Katie said. "We're going to have to get Grandpa to make the cookies."

"I know," Obie said. He reached up and pulled off his wig and a piece of spiderweb that had gotten stuck there.

Katie reached over and helped him. "I'm going to tell him that we're having a school party," she said. "And I need to bring cookies."

"There's no school party this year," Obie said. "Remember? We're giving the money to UNICEF."

"So?" Katie said. "Grandpa won't know that."

Obie was quiet for a minute. And then he said, "Katie?"

"What?" she said.

"Do you think this is bad, what we're doing?" Obie asked.

"Having a haunted house?" Katie said.

"Yeah," Obie said. "That and . . . you know. Other things."

Katie looked down at her hands. She picked some old raggedy nail polish off one finger. She knew what Obie meant. They had been doing some not nice things. Like, they were having a party — well, not a party, but a sort of party, a haunted house — and Mom had said no Halloween kids underfoot this year. They were sneaking things out of the house without permission. They had told some lies and then some other lies, and now Katie was going to have to tell another one, a big one, to Grandpa. And then there was Tiffany, stupid, crybaby Tiffany. They hadn't invited her.

Katie sighed. Still, it was all Tiffany's fault. If she had just invited Katie, then they wouldn't have had to have a haunted house anyway.

"It's not bad," Katie said. She looked up from peeling her nail polish. "Not really."

"You sure?" Obie said.

"Yes," Katie said. "I'm sure."

Obie made a little face, and sort of sighed.

Katie sighed, too. "Sort of sure," she said.

13

A Big Fat Lie

But Katie wasn't really sure. Thinking it over at supper, she thought maybe they were being a little bit bad. It made her feel funny in her stomach. Then while they were eating, she got an even more worried feeling in her stomach because Grandma asked again about the candles. Grandma had gone to the store and bought some new candles for the jack-o'-lanterns. Still, she kept talking about the other ones and wondering where they'd gone.

After supper, Katie knew she had to

ask Grandpa to bake some cookies, and what if he said no?

And then, when she did ask him and he said yes, Katie got so worried that she felt sort of sick. Because she had told him a lie, a big fat lie.

When it was time to go to bed, her stomach hurt so much she couldn't get to sleep.

She got up and tiptoed down the hall and into Obie's room.

"Obie!" she whispered. "Obie, it's not a monster. It's me, Katie."

Obie was buried under his covers, and he didn't answer.

"Obie," she whispered again. She sat down on the bed and tugged at his covers. "Obie, wake up. It's me, Katie. NOT a monster."

But Obie didn't answer. He was breathing heavily, almost snoring.

She pulled the covers off his head. "Obie?" she whispered.

Obie was sound asleep.

"Come on, Obie!" she said. She poked him just a little on his cheek.

He didn't wake up.

She leaned over and blew a little breath on his face.

He put a hand up and brushed at his face, and then turned over. Still asleep. Sound asleep.

Katie sat there a minute. She made a face at his back. What good was a twin brother if he wouldn't even wake up when she needed him?

She got up and went back down the hall.

She stopped for a minute at the top of the stairs. Downstairs, she could hear the quiet sound of Grandma and Grandpa talking. She could hear Grandpa's favorite music playing. He liked fancy music. He called it classical music. Katie didn't like classy music, though. She thought it was boring.

She sat down on the top step anyway, listening.

She missed Mom and Daddy.

She wished they were here. Daddy would know how she was feeling.

She sighed and put a hand on her stomach. The feeling was getting worse.

Daddy told her once about a guilty conscience. He said it made you feel bad. And sometimes, he said, it made you blush — like if someone asked did you do something and you said no but you did.

He said that meant you had a guilty conscience.

Katie put a hand on her face now.

It was hot. Was she blushing?

Did a guilty conscience make you feel this bad?

Suddenly Katie had an idea. She knew who could help. Her other grandma. Once, when Katie was very mad at her family, she was going to run away and live with her other grandma. Other grandma said she could, too.

Quietly, Katie got up and tiptoed down the hall to Mom's room. She went over to the phone by the bed. Very quietly, she

picked it up. She knew Grandma's number by heart, and she dialed it.

But nobody answered. It just rang and rang and rang.

Katie blew out her breath, then put the phone down and went back to the stairs.

First she sat on the top step. Then she moved down to next to top. And then next to next to top. She wanted to be far enough down to see into the living room, to see Grandma and Grandpa. She was really feeling very lonely.

When she got far enough down, she leaned through the railing bars and peeked into the living room. Grandma and Grandpa were laying out a jigsaw puzzle.

Katie leaned out farther to see better. The railing squeaked.

Katie backed up. But not quick enough.

Grandpa looked up and saw her. "Katie!" he said.

"I couldn't sleep," Katie said quickly.

"What's wrong?" Grandma asked,

turning to her. "Are you sick?"

Katie felt her lip quivering. "Mom makes me hot milk when I can't sleep," she said.

Grandma got up. "In that case," she said, "I'd better go make some right away. You come down here and sit with Grandpa while I do that."

Katie scooted down the stairs and into the living room.

She went and stood by Grandpa. He put an arm around her and pulled her close to him. "What's up, Toots?" he said, using the favorite name for her that Daddy used.

Katie shrugged. "Not much."

Grandpa pulled her onto his lap and stroked her hair. "Miss your mom and dad?" he said.

Katie nodded.

"Everything else all right?" Grandpa asked.

Katie shook her head. "I feel a little sick," she whispered.

"You do?" Grandpa said. "What hurts?"

Katie didn't answer. But then she said, very quietly, "I maybe did something bad."

"Oh," Grandpa said. "I see."

"But just one thing," Katie said. "Or two. Maybe three."

Grandpa patted her hair again. "I'm sure it's not bad enough to feel sick over," he said. "Is it?"

Katie thought over the things inside her head. Candles. Lies. A big fat lie to Grandpa! No invitation for crybaby Tiffany.

"It's kind of bad," she said.

"Know what helps me?" Grandpa said. "Telling somebody."

"I am," Katie said. "I'm telling you."

"No," Grandpa said. "I mean telling the person you did the bad thing to. Like, if you told someone a lie, you go back and tell them it was a lie. If you hurt somebody's feelings, you go and apologize."

"If you didn't invite them to the

haunted house, you go and invite them?" Katie asked.

Grandpa was quiet a minute. And then he said, "It would probably be a good idea."

Katie thought about it. She wasn't sure it was a good idea. She also thought it would be a really, really bad idea to tell Grandpa about the lie she had told him. He'd be so sad. She leaned her head back against his shoulder. But even if she didn't tell, just sitting there on his lap made her stomach feel a little bit better.

Just One More

The next morning, Katie was up very early making an invitation. For Tiffany. She wrote the same thing on it that Obie had on the other invitations:

Come to are Hunted hous.

But when she got to the part about refreshments served, she didn't know how to spell it, so she waited for Obie to wake up. He should make one on his computer like the other ones. She didn't want to give Crybaby an invitation with bad spelling.

When she was finished, she tiptoed downstairs. Nobody was awake yet, and it was just beginning to be light out. She unlocked the back door and went outside. She wanted one last look at the haunted house, since the next day was Halloween and everyone would be coming.

It was warm out that morning, and Katie was barefoot. As she tiptoed across the grass, she found it was very wet, and her feet felt pretty cold. By the time she got to the shed, her nightgown was also very wet around the bottom.

She stood at the door of the shed, looking in.

She smiled. Perfect, she thought, perfectly scary. Even in daylight, it was scary. There were candles, and the spiderwebs looked scary and the skeleton looked scary and the black cat on the windowsill looked very scary.

And then Katie saw something that for a minute was even more scary. A cat, a real cat, sat in the middle of the table. It was a fat orange and yellow cat, with its eyes half closed, squinched up, like it was mad at her.

"Whose cat are you?" Katie said. She backed up a little. "Shoo!" she said. "Get out of here."

The cat didn't get out. It just stared back at her, its tail twitching.

Katie backed up further. She didn't mind cats. She even liked some cats. But this one seemed bossy.

"Get!" she said.

The cat didn't move.

"I'll lock you in here," Katie said. "Then see how you feel."

But she didn't close and lock the door.

Instead she left the door open the way she and Obie always left it, and turned and headed back to the house. She had one last thing to do. And it was something even scarier than strange cats.

She let herself back into the house.

It was still very quiet, no one up and around at all.

Quietly, she tiptoed across the kitchen

to the drawer by the stove. It was where Mom and Daddy kept the matches.

Very quietly, Katie slid open the drawer.

She put her hand in. She stopped. She turned and looked all around the kitchen.

No one. No one was up yet.

She turned back to the drawer and reached in again. Matches, lots of them. She picked up one pack. Then another.

They felt strange in her hand, scary or something.

Her heart was beating hard, and that worried feeling was back in her stomach.

It was bad to play with matches, she knew. But this wasn't playing. This was important. And she'd be super careful. Besides, how else could she get the candles lit?

She stood looking at the matches in her hand.

She read the words on the matchbox: Close cover before . . . Before something. She couldn't read the last word.

For a long time, she stood looking at the matches.

She rubbed one foot on the other, rubbing off the grass bits that were stuck to her feet.

That bad feeling in her stomach got even worse.

She thought of what Grandpa had said last night — that if you did something bad, it helped to tell about it. She began to smile. So she'd just take the matches, and then tell about it later — after Halloween was already over.

But then she had another thought: What if she didn't do anything bad? Then she wouldn't have to tell about it, because there'd be nothing to tell. And matches, she knew, were really, really bad.

Katie turned the pack of matches over and over in her hand, thinking. The candles would look really cool lit up in the night. They would, wouldn't they?

She looked again at the matches. She

let out a big, fat breath. And then she put the matches back and closed the drawer. Hard.

She smiled to herself. Nothing bad to tell now. She and Obie would use the flashlight they had bought, that was all. She'd get the candles and bring them back in the dining room where they belonged, every single one of them. She'd bring back the candle holders, too. Grandma could stop worrying.

Which is exactly what Katie was in the middle of doing. When Grandpa came downstairs and found her doing it.

15

Caught

"Katie!" Grandpa said.

"Oh," Katie said. She sucked in her breath and turned around.

Grandpa was on his crutches, standing at the door to the dining room, watching her. She had just dumped a bunch of candles onto the table. She had piled them all up in the skirt of her nightgown and brought them back into the house, candle holders and all.

She moved over in front of the candles, hoping Grandpa wouldn't see them. "Oh," she said again. "Oh, hi, Grandpa."

"Hi, Katie," he said.

He didn't say anything more.

Katie didn't, either. She wiped her hands on her nightgown. Candles were kind of sticky. She rubbed one foot on top of another. Her feet were kind of sticky, too, with the wet grass on them.

"Katie?" Grandpa said.

"Umm?" she answered. She looked past Grandpa out the window.

It was beginning to get brighter out, the sun shining through the trees. Katie thought of the *Sesame Street* song: *Sunny day sweepin' the clouds away* . . . She began to hum it out loud.

"Katie?" Grandpa said again. "Stop singing."

"I'm not singing," Katie said.

"You're not?" Grandpa said. "What do you call it then?"

"Humming," Katie said.

"Stop humming, then," Grandpa said.

"Okay," Katie said.

"And look at me," Grandpa said.

Katie looked at him. She put her hands

on her hips. "What?" she said. She knew she sounded mad.

She wasn't mad. Just a little scared.

"Where did those candles come from?" Grandpa said.

"Candles?" Katie said. She shrugged. "Those candles?"

"Yes, those candles!" Grandpa said. His voice got a little mad-sounding.

"Oh," Katie said. She looked at the table. "Those candles."

She looked out the window again. She shrugged.

"Katie?" Grandpa said.

Katie could feel her lip quivering. "Out there," she said. She nodded with her head toward the window. "They came from out there."

"Outside?" Grandpa said.

Katie nodded.

"Why, Katie?" Grandpa said. "And where outside?"

Katie chewed on her bottom lip to keep it from quivering any more. She swallowed hard. "In the haunted house," she said.

"What haunted house?" Grandpa said. And then he said, "Oh! The one you didn't invite that girl to?"

Katie nodded.

"Wait a minute," Grandpa said. "The candles were in the haunted house, you said?"

Again Katie nodded.

"So where's the haunted house?" Grandpa said.

Katie sighed. She looked at Grandpa. "I'll go upstairs to get dressed. Then I'll show you."

A few minutes later Katie returned. "Follow me," she said.

Grandpa Knows

Katie and Grandpa stood at the door to the shed, looking in.

Katie held her breath. Her heart was going really fast. Was Grandpa going to be mad?

Maybe. But it wasn't really bad to have a haunted house, was it? Nobody had said no haunted house. Not exactly. They just said nobody underfoot and . . .

She looked up at Grandpa, watched him looking over the decorations — the spiderwebs, the skeleton, the coffin–toy box, the fake black cat. And the real live cat, who

was now stretched out in the middle of Obie's play table.

"Well, if this isn't something!" Grandpa said. He didn't sound mad. In fact, he sounded happy, pleased-like. "It *is* a haunted house!" he said. "Very good and scary-looking."

Katie smiled and took a deep breath. "Then you're not mad?" she said.

"Why would I be mad?" Grandpa said. "This is a wonderful haunted house. You did a great job."

"*We* did," Katie said. "Obie and me did it."

"It's wonderful!" Grandpa said. "Is that cat part of it? Whose cat is it?"

"He's not part of it," Katie said. "He's just some dumb cat that showed up this morning."

"Well, he's very effective," Grandpa said. "What's the toy box for?"

Katie grinned. "It's a coffin. Come see."

She went inside the shed, and Grandpa

swung himself in on his crutches.

"Wait till you see this," Katie said. She took the wig and fangs and bloody claw out of the toy box and held them out. "Obie puts these on and climbs in the box. Then he acts like he's just coming awake after being dead and he makes really scary noises."

"I'd like to see that," Grandpa said. He smiled at Katie. "Who's coming to this haunted house? And when?"

Katie looked down at her bare feet. "Just some people," she said. "Before trick or treat tomorrow night, Halloween night."

"What people?" Grandpa said.

Katie still didn't look up. "Just some people from school," she said.

"But not what's-her-name?" Grandpa said.

Katie nodded. "Tiffany. Crybaby Tiffany." She looked up at Grandpa. "But I made her an invitation before."

He smiled at her. "You did? Good for you."

Katie shrugged. She wasn't sure it was

good for her. But it did make the bad feeling in her stomach go away.

"Well, what are you going to feed your friends?" Grandpa asked. "If people come, you'll want to give them some refreshments, won't you?"

"That's what Obie said, too," Katie said.

"Well, suppose I make some extra cookies?" Grandpa said. "That's why I got up so early anyway, to make the ones for your school party. I'll make extras for the haunted house."

Katie didn't answer for a minute She stared at her feet, then up at the bossy cat. It was stretched out all over the table, like it owned the place.

"Grandpa?" she said. "You don't have to make any for school. We're not having a party."

"No Halloween party?" Grandpa said. "How can a school not have a Halloween party? Did you kids get in trouble or something?"

Katie shook her head. "No," she said. "We voted. We're giving our money for the party to UNICEF instead. And you know what, Grandpa?"

"What?" he said.

Katie took a deep breath. Then she said, "IsaidIwantedcookiesforschoolbutit wasreallyforthehauntedhouse."

Grandpa blinked. "Could you say that again?" he asked.

Katie took another deep breath. "I said, I didn't need cookies for school, I just told you that so you'd make them for the haunted house."

"Oh," Grandpa said. "Well. But why couldn't you just ask me to make them for the haunted house?"

Katie peeled at her nail polish. "I thought maybe you'd say no," she said. "Remember the night before Mom and Daddy left, what they said? They said they didn't want anyone underfoot this Halloween."

Grandpa looked all around. "It seems to me nobody'll be underfoot way back here."

Katie smiled. "That's what I told Obie," she said.

"In fact," Grandpa said, "this is so hidden, how are your friends going to find their way back here?"

Katie frowned. She hadn't thought about that.

"I'll think about it," Grandpa said. "There should be a way to light a path back here, don't you think? Maybe with candles stuck in sand or something?"

Katie nodded. There should be a way. But she didn't want Grandpa to start thinking candles.

Grandpa took her by the hand and turned her around toward the house. Then he slipped the crutches under his arms. "Just one more thing," he said. "What's this business about the candles? The way they disappeared and then reappeared?"

"Nothing!" she said. "I took the candles. I brought them out here. But then I changed my mind."

"Changed your mind?" Grandpa said.

"Just this morning? How come?"

Katie made her breath come out big and huffy. "Grandpa!" she said. She turned and looked at him, her hands on her hips. "Grandpa, how would we light the candles?"

Grandpa shrugged. "Well, I don't know," he said. "I suppose you'd light them the way anybody else does, with matches . . ."

He paused. "Oh," he said.

"See?" Katie said.

"Good girl," Grandpa said.

"I know," Katie said. And she smiled.

Invitations!

As soon as Katie and Grandpa got back to the house, Katie ran upstairs to Obie's room. "Obie!" she said. "Wake up. Turn on your computer."

Obie groaned. "No," he said. He turned over and buried his head in his pillow.

"Come on!" Katie said. "I need you to make more invitations."

"Too early," Obie said.

"It's not!" Katie said. She went over and sat on his bed, pulling the pillow out from under him. She hit him on the back of the head with it, but not too hard. "Please wake

up?" she said. "It's almost time for school anyway."

"Is not," Obie said. "My alarm didn't go yet."

"*Almost* time, I said," Katie said. "Please? This is important."

Obie sat up. He rubbed his hands all over his face and his head, messing up his hair.

"You look like a monster," Katie said.

"Why do I have to wake up?" Obie said. He rumpled his hair some more.

"We need another invitation," Katie said.

"Oh," Obie said. "For who?"

"Crybaby," Katie said. She sighed.

Obie rubbed his face again. "Oh," he said again. "How come?"

"Just because."

Obie sighed and stood up. He kind of stumbled over to the computer. He was wearing new pajamas that were still a little big for him. He tugged the pants up higher, then sat down and turned on the computer.

"Make three, okay?" Katie said. "One for Crybaby, and one for Grandma and one for Grandpa. We forgot to invite them."

Obie looked at her, blinking, like he had finally waked up. "Grandma?" he said. "Grandpa?"

"Yeah," Katie said. "Grandpa knows."

She told him about what had happened, how Grandpa had found out. "And," she added, "he's not even mad."

"How come you told him?" Obie said. He sounded a little sad. "Why didn't you wait for me to show him?"

Katie shrugged. "I had to, I got caught, I told you. When I was putting the candles back."

"Oh," Obie said.

"Know why I put them back?" Katie said.

"Why?" Obie said.

"Because we shouldn't play with matches," Katie said.

"I knew that," Obie said.

"So make the invitations," Katie said.

"And not the airplane kind. Make the monster kind."

Obie got the computer and printer on, and in a minute the printer began sending out invitations, monster ones.

Katie took them as they came out of the printer. One, two, three . . . then more, four, five, and six.

"We don't need six!" Katie said. "Just three."

Obie just shrugged. "Maybe we need them," he said.

Katie squinched up her eyes at him. "Obie!" she said. "Who are these for?"

Obie didn't answer.

"Obie!" Katie said. "Are these for Sam and Matt and Baby-Child?"

Obie nodded. "Uh-huh," he said.

"Obie!" Katie said.

"They won't take over," Obie said. "I promise."

"Ha!" Katie said. "They always do. Anyway, Baby-Child will get too scared when he sees you in the coffin box."

"I won't make scary sounds at him," Obie said. "Just funny sounds."

Katie made a big, huffy breath. And then she made another huffy breath. But then she remembered what Mrs. Henry said: If you ask one, you should ask everybody.

Even if they were brothers and even if they were big pains?

"Okay," she said at last, but she still felt grumpy. But then she began smiling, because then she had another thought. "But you have to do something," she said.

"What?" Obie said.

"You'll do it?" Katie said.

Obie shrugged. "I guess," he said.

"Okay," Katie said, smiling. "When Crybaby gets here? I get to be the body in the toy box."